WALK
ON THE
WILD
SIDE

Text and illustrations © 2015 Nicholas Oldland

Kids Can Press acknowledges the financial support of the Government of
Ontario, through the Ontario Media Development Corporation's Ontario Book
Initiative; the Ontario Arts Council; the Canada Council for the Arts; and the
Government of Canada, through the CBF, for our publishing activity.

Published in Canada by
Kids Can Press Ltd.
25 Dockside Drive
Toronto, ON M5A 0B5

Published in the U.S. by
Kids Can Press Ltd.
2250 Military Road
Tonawanda, NY 14150

www.kidscanpress.com

The artwork in this book was rendered in Photoshop.
The text is set in Animated Gothic.

Edited by Yvette Ghione
Series design by Marie Bartholomew
Designed by Julia Naimska

This book is smyth sewn casebound.
Manufactured in Malaysia in 10/2014 by Tien Wah Press (Pte) Ltd.

CM 15 0 9 8 7 6 5 4 3 2 1

Library and Archives Canada Cataloguing in Publication

Oldland, Nicholas, 1972–, author, illustrator
Walk on the wild side / Nicholas Oldland.
(Life in the wild)

ISBN 978-1-77138-109-3 (bound)

I. Title. II. Series.

PS8629.L46W35 2014   jC813'.6   C2013-908163-1

Kids Can Press is a *Corus*™ Entertainment company

WALK ON THE WILD SIDE

Nicholas Oldland

Kids Can Press

There once was a bear, a moose and a beaver who loved adventure. But sometimes their competitive natures got in the way of having fun.

One sunny morning, the bear, the moose and the beaver decided it was a great day to climb a mountain.

To get to the mountain, they descended into a valley ...

Walked through a grassy field ...

ARE WE THERE YET?

Waded through a stream ...

And crossed a deep canyon.

DON'T LOOK
DOWN.

At the foot of the mountain, they stopped for a snack. Between mouthfuls, the bear, the moose and the beaver discussed ways to make their hike more interesting.

The beaver thought the best way to add some excitement was to make it a race.

I'M #1!

As soon as they finished their last bites, the three friends were off and running. The race was on!

Thanks to his long legs, the moose took
an early lead. But the beaver and the
bear followed right on his tail.

Then just as the moose rounded
a bend in the mountain path, a
boulder came tumbling down
toward him.

Fortunately, the moose jumped out of harm's way just in time.

Unfortunately, he had jumped over the side of the mountain.

AHHHHH!

When the beaver rounded the bend, the moose was out of sight. Worried that he had fallen behind, the beaver picked up his pace.

When the bear came running by, he heard the moose's cry for help. The bear followed the sound to the mountain's edge, where he saw the moose dangling from a tree branch.

HELP!

Fearlessly, the bear attempted a daring rescue.

Sadly, he failed.

WHOOPS.

Thanks to the moose's quick
reflexes, the bear's life was saved.

THANKS!

But now they were both
hanging on for their lives.

The moose and the bear's cries for help echoed up the mountain. The beaver followed their calls back down the path.

The beaver's
instincts kicked in.

He chewed down
a tree ...

Carved out a
few notches ...

ARGHHH!

And lowered the simple ladder
to the moose and the bear so
they could climb up.

Back on solid ground, the three friends realized their hike had become a little too exciting. If they were going to make it to the top of the mountain, a slower pace might be better.

And that's when
their hike became
truly interesting.

They explored
a dark cave ...

Discovered
a prehistoric
fossil ...

And helped one another
along the way.

At the end of the day, the bear, the moose and the beaver agreed that reaching the top of the mountain was great, but enjoying the journey together was even better.